LITTLE CRITTER'S MANNERS

by Gina and Mercer Mayer

W9-BSY-998

A Random House PICTUREBACK® Book

Random House New York

Little Critter's Manners book, characters, text, and images copyright © 1993, 1995, and 2020 Gina and Mercer Mayer
Little Critter, Mercer Mayer's Little Critter, and Mercer Mayer's Little Critter and Logo are registered trademarks and Little Critter Classics and Logo
is a trademark of Orchard House Licensing Company. All rights reserved. Published in the United States by Random House Children's Books, a division
of Penguin Random House LLC, 1745 Broadway, New York, NY 10019, and in Canada by Penguin Random House Canada Limited, Toronto. The stories
in this collection were originally published separately by Golden Books, an imprint of Random House Children's Books, New York, in 1993 and 1995.
Pictureback, Random House, and the Random House colophon are registered trademarks of Penguin Random House LLC.
Visit us on the Web! • rhcbooks.com • littlecritter.com
Educators and librarians, for a variety of teaching tools, visit us at RHTeachersLibrarians.com
ISBN 978-1-9848-3093-7 (trade)
Printed in the United States of America
10 9 8 7 6 5 4 3 2 1
Random House Children's Books supports the First Amendment and celebrates the right to read.

JUST SAY PLEASE

BY GINA AND MERCER MAYER

My teacher said that good manners are important. She also said that everyone in our class could use a little help with good manners.

We made a good manners chart. We took turns
telling the teacher what to put on it.

I said, "Cover your mouth and nose when you sneeze."
My dad told me that.

The teacher said that was a very good one.

The class went over everything on the list, one by one.

Remember to say, "Please."
I remember to say please when I want to stay up past my bedtime.

Remember to say, "Thank you."
I always remember to say thank you when I get what I want.

Take turns.
I take turns most of the time. But sometimes it's so hard to wait.

Don't interrupt when someone is talking.
I guess that's why Mom gets so mad when I talk to her while she's on the phone.

Share.
I didn't know *sharing* was good manners. I wonder if my sister knows about that.

If you bump into someone or step on someone's toe, say, "Excuse me."
I guess that keeps people from getting mad at you.

Don't put your
elbows on the table.
I didn't know *elbows*
were bad manners.

Say you're sorry when you
do something wrong.
I'm not too good at that.

Put your napkin
on your lap at the
dinner table.
I thought that was
just so silly.

My teacher said that we could go over the list every morning so that we could tell her what we did to show good manners.

I thought that was neat. I decided to try to
have good manners right away.

When I got home, I ran in the front door and
knocked my sister down. I said, "Excuse me."
That didn't help. She cried anyway.

I went to tell Mom.
She was talking on the phone. I forgot I'm not supposed to interrupt when someone is talking.
So I said I was sorry.

Boy, was she surprised! She didn't even get mad at me for interrupting.

When Dad came home,
I asked him to play a game
with me. He said he was
too tired.
I said, "Please."
But he still said, "No."

I guess good manners
don't always work.

At dinner I put my napkin on my lap.

My sister asked me why.

I said, "Because it's good manners."

Then my napkin fell on the floor.

My sister said, "You dropped your good manners."

When Mom passed the rolls, I remembered to say thank you.

Mom said my teacher was doing a great job teaching us good manners.

I even remembered to keep my elbows off the table. Dad didn't, though.

After dinner, I let my sister color my homework picture. I thought it was nice of me to share my homework.

The next day at school, we went over the good manners list.
We each told how we used good manners.

Only one other critter in my class had better manners than me.
She got a big sticker that said I HAVE GOOD MANNERS.
It was cool.

I'm working really hard to remember my good manners because my teacher gives out a sticker every day.

And I love to get stickers.

I'M SORRY

BY GINA AND MERCER MAYER

Whenever I do something wrong,
I just say, "I'm sorry."

I knocked my sister off her bicycle by accident.
I said, "I'm sorry."

I left my sister's jump rope at the park.
I said, "I'm sorry."
We had to walk all the way back to get it.

I used my brother's blanket for my Super Critter cape. It got dirty when I was playing outside. I said, "I'm sorry."

When I was playing hide-and-seek with my sister, I got tangled in the curtain and pulled it down. I said, "I'm sorry."

When I was trying to reach for my favorite book, I knocked all the other books down. I said, "I'm sorry."
Mom helped me put them all back.

Mom said, "The baby is napping,
so please play quietly."
I forgot to play quietly. I woke the baby.

I said, "I'm sorry."
Mom said, "Go play outside."

I didn't know the baby's bedroom window
was open. "I'm sorry, Mom," I said.

When I was playing football,
I got tackled in Mom's garden.
I said, "Sorry!"

Mom and Dad asked me to close my bedroom window
when it rained, but I forgot. I said, "I'm sorry."

I didn't empty my pockets before Mom washed my pants.
I said, "I'm sorry."

Mom said, "That's what you said last time."

I really wasn't sorry that I forgot to clean my room. I hate to do that.

But I really was sorry when I stepped in a mud puddle with my new shoes . . .

and that I didn't wash my hands before I picked up the baby's bunny.

But I was especially sorry that
I left the top off my ant farm.

At dinner, Dad put some broccoli on my plate. I said, "I'm sorry, I don't like broccoli."

Dad said, "I'm sorry, you have to eat some anyway."

I was kind of messy when I was taking a bath. I said, "I'm sorry."

Dad made me clean up the bathroom.

After I took apart my sister's dollhouse, I
couldn't put it back together. I said I was sorry.
My sister called Mom.

While Mom fixed the dollhouse,
I was supposed to watch my little
brother. Oops!

I said, "I'm sorry, Mom."
Mom said, "Sometimes saying
'I'm sorry' just isn't good enough."

I didn't know that.

If saying "I'm sorry" isn't good enough,
I guess I'll just have to be more careful.